*Bartholomew and the Morning Monsters*

Written by Sophie Berger
Illustrated by Ruan van Vliet

British Library Cataloguing-in-Publication Data.

A CIP record for this book is available from the British Library.
ISBN: 978-1-908714-84-8
First published in the UK, 2020 and USA, 2021

Cicada Books Ltd
48 Burghley Road
London, NW5 1UE
www.cicadabooks.co.uk

Printed in China

# BARTHOLOMEW AND THE MORNING MONSTERS

BY SOPHIE BERGER and RUAN VAN VLIET

Every night, the monsters had a
wild rumpus in Bartholomew's room.

It was so much fun, that in the morning, they didn't want to leave.

GOOD MORNING BARTHOLOMEW! TIME TO RISE AND SHINE!

This made waking up
very difficult.

UURGHH... I CAN'T!

Getting dressed was almost impossible.

Brushing teeth was a complicated procedure.

And other simple morning routines...

...just didn't go quite to plan.

BARTHOLOMEW! ARE YOU COMING?

Breakfast was, frankly,
a disaster.

Things that were right there a second ago, seemed to disappear without a trace.

And shoelaces…

Well, let's not even talk about the shoelaces.

Dad decided
it was time to step in.

LET'S SORT YOU OUT,
BARTHOLOMEW.

And finally...

against all odds...

Bartholomew made it out the door.

Ready for
the day to begin.